D1168166

This book belongs to:

_____

Published by Ladybird Books Ltd
27 Wrights Lane London W8 5TZ
A Penguin Company
3 5 7 9 10 8 6 4 2

Text © Karen Hayles MCMXCV Illustrations © Cliff Wright MCMXCV
© LADYBIRD BOOKS LTD MCMXCV
This edition MCMXCVI

Printed in Italy

The Star That Fell

by Karen Hayles
illustrated by Cliff Wright

Ladybird

One night a star fell...

Fox found the star first...

and she took it back to her den
so that her cubs would feel safe
in the dark.

Badger noticed the glow…

and he borrowed the star to light
his way through the inky wood.

Owl came across the star and
she flew it to a tall tree so that
she could see it from afar.

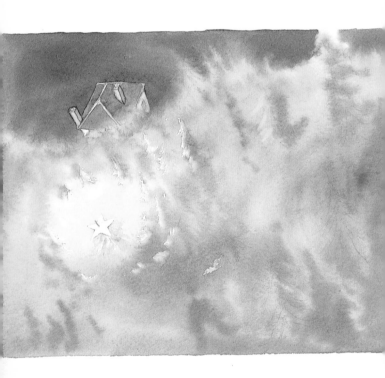

When Squirrel woke the
next morning…

she took her children to
see the wonderful star
that Owl had put at the
top of their tree.

Magpie stole the bright star…

and he hid it in his nest with all
the other glittering things.

Stag knocked the star from
the nest…

Rabbit found it soon afterwards.
She carried it back to her warren
to keep her babies warm.

Dog dug up the star…

and he gave it to his friend,
Maddy, as a gift.

Maddy ran home with the star...

and she put it in her secret box of
very special things.

But the star began to fade.

Maddy's father said the star
belonged to the sky and they
must give it back.

So that night Maddy opened her bedroom window and set the star free. Up… up… it zoomed into the dark sky, growing brighter and brighter as it went.

Now every evening before she goes to sleep, if the sky is clear and she looks very carefully, Maddy can see her star twinkling in its place amongst all the others... just where it always was.